HEARTBREAK DREAMS

Daniel Elijah Sanderfer

Mountain Ranch Publishing

Cover design by: Daniel Elijah Sanderfer
Printed in the United States of America

PROLOGUE

They say a heart can't dream. I beg to differ. I say a heart can dream. The heart is that inner being, it is who you are. It is more than the muscle which pumps your blood. A heart can feel. It can be both resilient and hard, unchanging. It can be broken a thousand times, yet we simple humans put it back together again and again and offer it to someone new. When our heart is broken the first time, we say we'll never love again. It's sad but true, we will likely never love again in the same way, we loved that first person.

What if for once, the first cut wasn't the deepest? What if our first love became our forever love? I'm not saying there won't be pain but just think of how much stronger you'll be if somehow you do make it, together. Just think of how much closer you'll be. Call me old-fashioned but I believe when things are broken you try to fix them. On the same note, I know some people will never change. In those cases, it's best just to make a clean break.

I hit the throttle on my four-wheeler and sped toward the country store. Mama made some extra tips at the diner today and told me to go treat myself. It was late in the afternoon when I hopped aboard with my mind set on getting an RC Cola and a candy bar… maybe a zero. It's the little things in life that make me happy.

Those moments are few and far between in a place like Harlan, Kentucky. There isn't a lot in this part of the county where we live. I guess we're one of the lucky ones though. Mama inherited the land our trailer is on from Grandma and Grandpa after they passed a few years ago. It's got a few acres nestled on a hillside with a little grassy drive that pulls up out front. There's also an old workshop on the land where granddad used to tinker about and another old trailer where he and grandma used to live. Mamas always said that one day she's gonna fix it up and rent it.

It's just us now… mama and me. For now, anyway. Daddy is always running off and leaving us to fend for ourselves. You see, he's got himself a little problem. He's been addicted to meth for years. Unfortunately, every time he runs out of money and comes back, mama accepts him with open arms. It's the way it's always been and the way it will always be. I suppose she'll love him till her dying day.

When he's straight, he usually works at autobody shops painting cars and he's actually really good at it. If you haven't figured it out by now, we're more than just a little country. We're straight-up white trash hillbillies and proud. Mama always taught me to never be ashamed of my roots and I never will be. We don't fly any rebel flags or shit like that though, because mama taught me it ain't right. She says people are people regardless of the color of their skin or who they love.

At my age, I'm ready to get the hell out of this

place as soon as possible. What kind of future does a seventeen-year-old boy got in a town that's boarded up and dying a slow death? Don't get me wrong, we've got a few little shops; a goodwill store, a Chinese restaurant, a Cato, and a Walmart. Most of the folks here rely on welfare and social security to get by. The ones who do work are stuck in no-end service jobs that have shitty pay.

Mama works at The Old Harlan Diner and it's exactly what you think. A shady little dive on the outskirts of town with a cook that smokes while he's cooking, and a bunch of ladies, mom's age, with kids that are just trying to get by. Her name is Loretta and we're pretty close. We didn't use to be until my daddy started beating her and I would stand between them and take the punches instead.

That's part of the reason mama took me out of school in the tenth grade. So, I could keep the house clean and keep an eye on things while she's working. Plus, the teachers had started calling to ask what had happened. I stayed home in case dad would try to sneak in there and take our stuff to pawn for his fix or to bring one of his lady friends over to play around with. With me there, he couldn't get away with that.

Thankfully, Mom's got an old Geo Metro that gets her back and forth to her job and gets us to town when we need something. The only nice thing daddy ever did for me was buy the old four-wheeler I cruise around on. Although, I think he actually traded his old pickup for it and some cash. I'm not supposed to drive it in town though. So, I just used it to get around here. Sometimes I go to the country store, or down to the old creek to sit and think. Every once in a blue moon, I'll take it up the road to borrow some sugar or something for mom.

Don't get me wrong. I know I've painted a pretty grim picture of life out here but it's not all that bad. We've got the Appalachian Mountains all around us and lots of beautiful nature. I know I'll miss that if I ever leave. One time when I was young, I went shopping with mama and grandma to Kingsport. It's just over a mountain or two south down in Tennessee but to a twelve-year-old, it was like going to New York City.

That's where I hope to move to someday. I'll get a good job in a nice body shop or something, maybe even an oil change place. I'll buy a little house in the suburbs and come back home for the holidays. Maybe I'll even get a pickup truck, one of those souped-up antique ones with a loud muffler. Maybe too, I'll be able to live my life without all these secrets and worries. You see, I've got myself a little problem. It's not really a problem as much as it is a secret. I like boys. I always have and always will. My mom doesn't know but I'd like to think she'd be relieved knowing that I'm nothing like my dad.

He used to try to influence me to be like him. He'd show me his Playboys and say, "Now, that's a woman! When you get sixteen, I'mma take you downtown and find you a woman like that who can teach you how to be a man."

I was appalled. No one can teach you how to be a man. You take the wisdom from the wise ones around you, do some thinking, then you become the man you want to be. I want to be a good man. I want to find a guy who is faithful and true, one that has the same hopes and dreams and wishes that I do. We'll work our jobs, then come home and greet each other with a kiss. Then, we'll fix dinner and watch reruns of The Andy Griffith Show before turning in. We'll be lovers, we'll be friends. Heck, every night will be like a sleepover that never ends.

That's one of the reasons I've got to get out of here. Lately, youthful stirrings have been driving me wild. Mama says they're just growing pains. I don't think so. I dream about the city all day. I dream about boys and sharing my first time with some lonesome cowboy just looking for a warm stranger to spend the night with. A few times, I've even thought about hanging out by the truck stop on the outskirts of town and seeing if some guy might want to hook up in the stalls.

I understand that's a little dangerous and extreme. You see my point though, right? I really need a boy and fast. I sat my RC and Zero bar on the counter as Ms. Jodie rang them up, "Oh, Waylon, how's Loretta? We been keepin' her in our prayers at church."

Ms. Jodie is larger than life in both size and personality. Daddy used to say she's got her finger on the pulse of the town.

"She's fine," I replied, "just workin' all the time."

"Any signs of your daddy?"

"No ma'am."

I paid for my snacks and started toward the door as she stood, "When are you gonna come visit us at the church?"

"I'll try one of these Sundays. You know how

busy things are at the house."

"Well, we'd love to have you!"

"Thanks, Ms. Jodie."

"Send your mama my love."

I rolled my eyes and sighed in relief as I high stepped it to my four-wheeler. Thank God I got away before she started asking about whether I had a girlfriend yet. Why does everyone always assume that someone wants to be in a relationship? It's like a requirement out here. Like the old sayin' goes, *"If you ain't married and got two kids by twenty-one, then you're probably gonna die alone."*

I was fumbling with my candy bar when I heard another four-wheeler approach. I lifted my eyes and squinted from under my cowboy hat. A silhouette emerged in the setting sun. Like a vision coming to fruition, a boy emerged from the haloed shadows. His face was void of expression. He was wearing tight blue jeans and a button-up flannel shirt with a white tank top underneath. I closed my mouth and swallowed hard as he sped by and tipped his hat.

I turned around and watched him sort himself as he got off. My body shivered. He looked to be about my age but I'd never seen him around before. I thought for a moment and tried to figure out who lived in the direction from which he came. The only person that lives out there is Mr. Creech, the old used car dealer that used to be in town.

I heard the bell jingle on the front door of the store and turned around again to see if it was the dream that had just drivin' by. It was! He popped the top on a can of mountain dew and took a long swig before wiping his lips on his shirt sleeve. I liked mine, wishin' I was that can his lips were pressed to. If not for just a moment, I'd sell my soul to taste him just once for just a few moments.

I closed my eyes and turned my attention to the road. It hurts too much to think about. It hurts too much to look at him. It hurts too much to be the only boy like me. It hurts too much that people can't just mind their own business and let folks be free to be whoever they want to be. I stiffened my upper lip and tried not to cry.

I headed back out to my four-wheeler and was about to start it up and head home when behind me, I heard his engine rev then come to a stop beside me. I froze in fear and braced myself to hear his voice for the first time.

"Hey."

I turned to him and nodded, "Hey."

"How far is town from here?"

"It's a pretty good way down the road there."

He sucked his teeth, "Damn, I've been going crazy since I got here."

"Where you from?"

"Oh, I'm from Harlan County. I used to live in town before mama and daddy sent me out here."

"Why'd they send you out here? That is if you don't mind me asking?"

He took another swig of his mountain dew and stared pensively at the mountains overhead, "I was gettin' into fights and shit. So, they sent me out here to live with my grandpa."

"Bummer."

"It was either this or military school."

I grinned. He was straight-up rough trade. One

of those city boys who just thinks he's country.

"I'm Scooter, by the way, Scooter James Creech. Everybody just calls me Scooter."

"Waylon... Waylon Trey Evarts," I smiled as I reached out to shake his hand.

"Creech? Any relation to Raymond Creech?"

"He's my Grandpa."

"I was about to say, didn't no one live out the way you came from except him."

"Yep, my folks say living in the boondocks will keep me out of trouble."

"That it will," I chuckled.

After we shook hands, we both turned our gaze to the mountains for a minute before he spoke again, "So, what's there to do out here?"

"Well, there's an old house that's falling down next to the creek. We could go explorin' or huntin' for arrowheads in the creek bed?"

"I'm game if you are?"

"I ain't got nothin' better to do. I just have to go by the house and tell mama."

"I'll go too," he crooned.

We shifted to prepare for takeoff. When I glanced back to see if he were ready, he gave me a nod. Inside my mind, I was freaking out. I'd never brought a boy home before. Come to think of it, I'd never brought anyone home before. My mind was lost as trees raced by. He came up alongside and shouted, "Let's race!"

I panicked for a moment. I wasn't even sure this old thing could race. His eyes were squinty and playful. Mine were serious and forlorn. However, I honored his request and kicked it into high gear. As the world raced by us, his eyes didn't leave mine but to occasionally check to make sure no cars were approaching on the little two-lane road.

Inside my chest, my heart was racing... its beats were thundering in my ears like the thumping of a drum. Blood was rushing through my veins like the water in the creek rushes during a mountain storm. For the very first time, I felt alive. I felt something I'd never felt before. There was some connection between Scooter and me... a feeling that we were kindred spirits who'd been searching for one another for years. Almost like brothers but without the barrier of blood to keep us from going too far.

Oh God, we were already living dangerously, driving fast down a road of no return. While he was caught up in the race, I was caught up in him. The way his chiseled jawline curved to a cleft chin. The way his blue-green eyes were all squinty in the shadowed light of the near-setting sun. The way his jeans and shirt clung to his body like cellophane. It was as if he'd been poured into them. It was all too much and yet I couldn't get enough. I swear to God if I ever get the chance, I'll kiss him good. I'll kiss him the way a man should kiss another man... with just the right amount of pressure and passion.

I reached to adjust my cock. It was about to bust through the zipper of my jeans. I realized too that we were fast approaching my road and started to hit the brakes. He did the same and veered off the highway with me down a dirt footpath with grass growing down the center. A moment later, we were in front of my trailer and we dismounted. I got lost watching him adjust himself and shouted, "We're here."

It was a little louder than I'd intended but my ears were still in tune with the motor of my four-wheeler. "I'll be right back."

I rushed inside to find mama washing dishes in the kitchen. She dried her hands and met my gaze, "I was about to send a search party. What took so long?"

"Mama… I met a boy at the gas station. He's new in town and I was wonderin' if I could go down to the creek with him and hunt for arrowheads."

"Just be back before dark."

"Yes ma'am."

I rushed back outside, letting the screen door slam as I did. Scooter was leaning up against his four-wheeler and gazing out across the land. A sudden feeling of nervousness washed over me as I stood beside him. "It's nice out here," he mumbled.

"Yeah, it really is."

"Quiet."

"Mm-hmm."

"Mama said we could go but I have to be back before dark."

"Cool," he nodded before turning to meet my gaze. "You lead the way. I don't know my way around these parts."

I rushed to my ride and hopped on. He did the same, then we were off again. Back up the driveway we started before I took a sharp turn down a hill and towards the woods on the lower part of our land. Once we arrived, I got off and stood for a moment. "This is my favorite spot on the land. I come down here a lot to think and get away from it all."

He smiled, then wrapped an arm around my

neck. “You know what, Waylon? I think you and are gonna be great friends.”

Nothing in this world could have felt better than having his arm around me as we gazed at that little creek just rolling by. Maybe we’d never be more than just buddies but I was certain at that moment, he was going to be the boy I secretly loved and lusted after until my dying day. He’d probably eventually marry some girl and break my heart but he’d never know. That is unless fate intervened and saw it fit that he and I should be we. Sigh, a boy can dream I suppose.

HEARTBREAK DREAMS

DANIEL ELIJAH SANDERFER

PART ONE

"Found one," he shouted as he held it up.

I rushed over to look and confirmed, "Yep, it sure is."

"Can I keep it?"

"Of course."

He tucked it into his pocket before starting back towards the bank. I followed and plopped down in the tall grass to enjoy my RC and Zero bar. "Want some?" I offered.

"Nah, I'm good."

We sat in silent reflection before he broke it, "This is nice… but before this goes any further, I think you should know why I was gettin' into fights and stuff back in town."

I listened as he continued, "You see, I ain't like other boys. Daddy says there's something wrong with me but mama says it's just the way God made me. Those boys in school used to corner me in the bathroom, beat me up, and call me a faggot."

"Whatever for?"

"Because I got caught checking out one of their butts."

"So, you're…"

He held up his hand, "I ain't one for labels but I am who I am. I know that now.

I could hardly contain my excitement as my lips formed a grin, "Scooter... you and I have a lot more in common than you might think."

"How so?"

I took a swig of my RC, "Well, I like guys too."

His eyes looked dreamy as he whispered, "Is that so?"

"Yeah... it is."

Just when I thought he might lean in for a kiss, he shifted then stood. "I best be gettin' back. Papa will get worried if I'm not in before dark."

"I better get back too," I sighed.

Although, I could have sat there on that creek bank till the end of time with him. Somehow, by some strange twist of fate, we'd found one another. For once in my wretched life, something went right. I know not every gay boy is compatible but he was the stuff my wet dreams were made of.

On the way back to the four-wheelers, I was a few steps ahead when he reached to grab my hand. I turned to meet his gaze and found him searching for words. "Waylon... I... um... It's nice to know I'm not alone out here."

"Likewise," I smiled.

I waited again to no avail and watched as he hopped aboard his four-wheeler and started it up. "Maybe we can meet here tomorrow... same time?"

"I'd like that."

He gave me a nod, "Goodnight, Waylon."

"Goodnight, Scooter."

After a pensive drive home, I pulled up outside the trailer and rushed inside. "What are you so happy about?" Mama asked curiously.

"Oh, just my new friend, Scooter. He's Mr. Creech's grandson."

"Your father and I bought our first pickup from Mr. Creech... it was a good one. Lasted for years before the asshole wrecked it."

I rolled my eyes, "Do we have to talk about him tonight?"

Mama shook her head, "I'm good... let's just eat dinner and watch some Andy Griffith,"

"Sounds like a plan," I replied as I pulled up a chair at our weathered Formica table.

SCOOTER

Grandpa was sitting at the kitchen table eatin' a bowl of beans when I came in. "Where you been, boy?"

"Down by the creek with a friend."

I pulled the arrowhead from my pocket and set it on the table in front of him. He picked it up and gave it a once over, "That's a nice one... glad to see you staying out of trouble."

I rolled my eyes. If he only knew that I wasn't the one makin' trouble. I was just trying to defend myself. In the winter, I'll be eighteen and I plan on hitting the road and never looking back. Since I got here, I've been keeping myself busy with chores and biding time.

I'll never understand why if the boys can check out the girls, why I can't check out boys. We all need to feel safe. We all need to feel normal. At least if I can't have a boy of my own, the least I should be allowed is a glance. Unfortunately, these dudes are so fragile in their masculinity that they can't take a glance as a compliment. In all honesty, they just don't like the idea of being treated how they treat their girls.

I'll get off my soapbox now and quit boring you. Isn't life funny? I never thought I could meet a boy like Waylon... like me. He's not your stereotypical gay. He's a guy's guy like myself. A sturdy-built country boy with an accent as thick as gravy and body as slender as a willow. What I'd give to see him naked.

Before I came out here, there wasn't really anywhere I could go in the city to sit and think or whittle away an afternoon. At grandpa's though, he's got a big junkyard with tons of rusted-out old cars. I like to go out there and sit inside them and dream of a life far away from here.

I could tell you where most of these old cars came from. I used to ride with him down to Kingsport and Johnson City, when I was younger, to pick up old junkers. I remember being mesmerized by all the stores and opportunities. All the people just going about their daily lives. All the tidy little boxes in a row with their well-manicured yards. I'll always be country as apple pie but I can't deny that it would be nice to live somewhere like that.

I'm young and alive and want to make a name for myself. I want to have all the opportunities and chances other guys like myself have. I want to see a gay bar. Have a drink with some cowboys like me. Dance to some old Loretta Lynn on the jukebox with my guy. I know I can never do that here. That's why I have to pull up stakes and leave. What I didn't count on was meeting someone like me... here of all places.

WAYLON

Mama turned in after dinner. She had to work the breakfast shift tomorrow. I decided to go outside and sit on the covered porch for a while. The brief thought that I wished Scooter were here crossed my mind. It'd be nice to have someone to keep me company. I get so lonely sometimes that I can't stand it. My heart burns to be with someone. My lips salivate to conversate with someone like-minded. My body longs to be snuggled up to another so I can hear him breathe. To know someone's watching over me. I want to know safety and peace with someone.

I wiped my nose on my shirt sleeve and sniffled. I couldn't wait to see Scooter again tomorrow. Tonight, I'll hold him in my dreams until I could finally do so in person. Tonight, I'll hold him in my hand as I get lost thinking of his heart beating next to mine. In the morning, mama was already gone by the time I got awake. I stumbled around the house for a bit before getting started with my chores.

The bad thing about waiting is it gives the mind too much time to wander and play. Even after mom got home, I was practically hyperventilating while trying to make sure everything was perfect. Everything from my hair to the clothes I was wearing. It all had to be perfect for him.

I was waiting on the porch when mama came up from behind, "This boy must be something real special to have you all worked up like this."

I turned to her with a curious expression,

"What do you mean?"

She grinned, "Come off it, don't act like I don't know."

"Know what?"

"That you're different."

I covered my face, "Mom, do we really have to do this right now."

"Well, I'm just sayin' you ain't never showed interest in girls. So, I just assumed you went the other way."

"Please don't hate me for it."

She shook her head and closed her eyes, "Baby, all I care about is that you're safe and happy. It doesn't mean a hill of beans whether you like boys or girls... just don't be like your father."

"Trust me, I could never be like him."

She took a seat in a rocking chair and continued, "I just want to say one more thing. You know as well as I do that people around these parts don't take too kindly to people of the same sex being romantic... so y'all keep it on the down-low if you go anywhere public."

"You don't have to worry about that mom, we're just getting to know each other right now."

"That's good... you don't have to be in a rush to fall in love or get laid."

"Mom, please," I groaned.

She stood and giggled, "Well, do I at least get to meet him?"

"If you must, but then you have to go back inside!"

"Hey, this is my house and I'll do whatever I damn well please."

"Yes, ma'am."

"I just want to be able to identify him if he hurts you in any way."

"What do you mean?"

"I don't need to tell you about these small-minded bigots that live around here. All I'm sayin' is he better not lay a hand on you or put you in danger."

The sound of a motor humming and tires on gravels echoed through the hollow. "That's him! That's him!"

Mom giggled, "Calm down, Mary. You look fine."

He pulled up in front of the porch in his blue jeans and tank top like yesterday but with no over-shirt this time. Mom glanced at me and arched a brow. "He looks a little rough, love."

"All the boys around here look rough, mom!"

She rolled her eyes as he made his way up the steps and extended his hand, "Hi, I'm Scooter."

"Loretta, Waylon's mom."

I smiled at him and he did the same to me, "She just wanted to meet you before we left."

"That's fine. I understand completely. Grandpa said I had to be home before nightfall."

"Same rules here," mom added.

I walked with him down the stairs and took my place on my four-wheeler. Mom leaned over the rail, "Ya'll be careful now, you hear?"

"Yes ma'am," we replied in unison before

speeding off.

I turned to start down the bank that leads to the hollow and he shouted, "Wait."

He came up alongside and hesitated for a moment. "Why don't I show you my thinking spot today?"

"Okay," I smiled shyly. "Should I just follow you?"

He suddenly looked nervous as he replied, "Actually, why don't you just hop on mine? I'll bring you home in time."

"Okay."

I hit the throttle to go back to the driveway, then dismounted after turning it off.

SCOOTER

On the way back, I got lost watching him walk. It was a distinctive lazy shuffle. I could see the dust from the dirt road rise as he kicked his feet. His hands were tucked into the pockets of his jeans. I knew he was as nervous as me. I put on a confident expression as he threw his leg over and scooted close to me. I was trying not to think about how awesome it was to have another boy so close to me. Momentarily, I wondered if he was gonna put his arms around me or rest them on the rear cargo rack.

To my disappointment, he rested them on the rear rack. "You on?"

"Yeah."

I took off in the direction of Grandpa's and tried to think of ways to get him to touch me.

Up around the bend in the road would be my best chance. I took the curve hard and bit my bottom lip as I hit the gas. His arms came around my waist and held on tight. I could feel his fingers digging into my abs and tightened on them. A smile wiped across my face as I felt his head come to rest on my back. What I'd give to know what he was thinking? Did he really like me or was he just holding on? Did he think I was as cute as I thought he was?

All these questions were swirling around in my head like a hurricane when I turned onto the graveled road that led to Papaw's. He'd gone into town for dinner tonight, so Waylon and I would have the whole junkyard to ourselves. I could show him my favorite cars and maybe we could lay in an old truck bed and watch the clouds go by before sunset. It wasn't anything fancy but maybe, just maybe a boy like him would find this place as romantic as I did.

We pulled into the center of the field and dismounted. Although, I could have driven that old Honda forever if I'd have known he would've been holding me the whole trip. He gazed around and grinned before meeting my gaze, "What is this place?"

"The junkyard."

His expression dampened, "My daddy would have loved to have fixed some of these up."

"Does he like cars?"

"Well, he used to before he got hooked on that crud."

"Oh, I'm sorry."

"It's okay. I just have to remember the man he is now isn't who he really is."

I took a toothpick from my pocket and gripped it between my teeth. "I find that most people don't change when they get hooked on that stuff. A few of the guys from school got into that. Most of em' are either in jail or dead now."

"That's effed up."

"Yeah… it is."

"Papaw always says people are responsible for their own choices… whether they're good or bad. Personally, I like to see the best in people until they do something to wrong me."

"Yeah," he sighed, "I used to feel that way about dad until he stormed in one night when he was coming down. He started throwing stuff and tearing the house apart for something he could sell to get a fix. When mama tried to stop him, he just threw her to the side. I was hollering and screaming for him to stop, but he just started layin' into me and tellin' me to shut up."

I tightened my jaw and glanced away. What he was telling me made me want to hunt the man down and kill him. How anyone could lay his hands on someone as beautiful as Waylon to hurt him, was beyond me. How anyone could lay a hand on anyone to hurt them was beyond me. Just like those dudes that cornered me in the bathroom and beat me up, all I remember thinking was why? What had I done so wrong to deserve this?

It doesn't matter now. Some people have issues that can only be worked out in time or therapy. Mom and dad tried to send me to therapy when they found out the reason I was getting beat up. However, I just sat there with my arms crossed and refused to talk. What's some backwoods Freud wannabe gonna tell me about being gay. Especially one that goes to church with mama and daddy. Psychiatry mixed with religious propaganda isn't therapy. Telling a boy who likes other boys that he needs to go off to the city and see a conversion specialist to turn him straight is quackery at its finest.

I'm not gonna sit here and say that when I first figured out who I was that I wasn't scared and upset. Eventually, though, I grew to accept that I was different. Thank God I was able to find a book at the library and do research on the internet that helped me to realize gay was ok. Also, the fact that just because I'm gay doesn't mean I have to wear makeup and carry a purse. I'm not a girl or a sissy. I just happen to be a dude that likes dudes. I almost got in trouble when I stumbled onto some picture sites with trucker guys and factory workers nude. I don't have to tell you that I was both fascinated and turned on more than I've ever been in my life.

I only wish in those times of self-exploration that mom and dad would have had internet so I could research things further. Maybe someday when I get to the big city, I can go to one of those dirty bookstores and buy me some magazines like the ones I saw advertised on that website... that is if my boyfriend doesn't mind. Better yet, maybe he and I can explore some roleplay and dress up together. I got lost for a minute picturing Waylon in tight faded blue jeans and a cut-off flannel shirt.

Thankfully, he was lost staring at all the cars and old machinery so I could adjust myself before he saw my boner. When he turned back around, he asked, "So, what do you want to do first?"

"I thought we'd drive to the back of the property. There's an old pickup truck back there where I hang out. When it's nice, I just lay in the back and watch the clouds go by."

"That sounds awesome," he said with a smile.

We hopped back aboard my four-wheeler and I headed toward the back. "Nobody else knows about this place," I shouted.

"Don't worry... I can keep a secret."

Something about the way he said it made my heart sigh. Just like his creek, this place would be our little secret. A place where we could escape the heteronormative world and just be two boys in love. Well... in lust for right now. It's just the second day we've known each other. I can't have us runnin' off and gettin' married yet. Even though I've already thought about it half a dozen times since we'd met.

In the back of the junkyard sits an old 67 Chevy. It's a faded blue and rusted out on the sides. I'd pulled some old carpet from an old mobile home to lie in the back and some old couch pillows to make it more comfortable. Waylon sat on the tailgate and glanced around. "Nice setup you got here."

I climbed aboard and propped my hands behind my head. "Yeah, it suits me well."

I had my eyes closed when I replied but after I finished, I couldn't help but ask, "Wanna come up here with me?"

He flashed me a smile and replied with a meek, "Okay."

After getting comfortable, I couldn't deny how nice it was to be lying side by side with him. My senses were alive and my nerves were on end. When I was a kid and went to church, I remember the reverend speaking about a road to temptation. If there were such a road, we'd just found where it ended. Who'd have thought it would be the back of a beat-up 67 Chevy in my grandpa's junkyard?

I'd dreamed of this very scenario. I'd had furious wack-off sessions fantasizing about it. Now, here I was with a super-hot boy and it was everything I could do to keep from being less than a gentleman and making a move.

In an attempt to divert ourselves from the obvious tension, I asked, "Where do you see yourself when you get older?"

"Anywhere but here," he laughed.

"Same here," I laughed too.

"That one looks like an old Trans-Am," he pointed to the sky.

I searched for a moment, "What do you know? It sure does."

He let out a soft sigh and continued on the conversation I'd initiated a moment ago. "I want to move to the city. Get a good job. Maybe find a little place in the suburbs."

"Get out," I rolled over, "Me too."

"Really?" He smiled.

"Really!"

Slowly, he moved his hand and wrapped it around two of my fingers. "I really like you, Scooter."

I moved my fingers to intertwine them with his, "I like you too, Waylon."

Our faces began drifting closer and our eyes became heavy. I was all too ready to know if his lips tasted as delicious as they looked when a voice shouted from across the junkyard. "Scooter James! Scooter James Creech, where are ya boy?"

"Shit," I whispered as Waylon attempted to compose himself.

We'd gotten so lost in one another's eyes that we hadn't noticed it was getting dark. We separated our hands, jumped out of the truck, and started running back toward the front of the junkyard. The whole way, my heart was racing and I couldn't help but feel so disappointed that we didn't get to do what we were about to do.

Papaw was standing with his hand perched on his brow and glancing around when I emerged and shouted, "We're here… I was just showin' Waylon the junkyard."

"I thought I told you not to go out in there. One of y'all could've gotten hurt."

"We were real careful, sir, I promise."

"Well, as long as y'all didn't get hurt. I ain't

about to have to run one of you boys to the hospital for a tetanus shot if ya get cut or something." He pointed his cane, "Who's this?"

"This is Waylon, Papaw. He lives up the road a ways."

Waylon extended his hand, "My mom and dad used to buy all of their cars from you when you were in business."

"Well then," Grandpa smiled.

Inside, I was super happy he said that. Grandpa always likes to meet people who remembered his business. His car lot was his life but after a heart attack and a few strokes, he isn't able to do much anymore. I was certain he was okay with grandpa now, which meant a lot to me. He may not know all the details of my life but he respects that I'm different and that it wasn't my fault I got sent out here to live with him.

I think in their mind, my parents thought sending me out here would keep me from acting on my homosexual desires. How funny is it that I would meet another boy like me out here in this wilderness? It just goes to show you that God doesn't make mistakes. I am who I am and if he'd have wanted me to be something different then he'd have made me that way.

Grandpa turned his gaze back to the house and crooned, "I best get on in and you best be gettin' that boy back home. I'm sure his folks'll be worried if he's out past dark."

"It was nice to meet you," Waylon interjected

and threw up a hand as Grandpa started back to the house.

Once he was gone, Waylon turned his gaze to the ground and traced the dirt with his foot. "I suppose he's right, but can we see each other again tomorrow?"

"I was hopin' you'd ask that."

He lifted his eyes, "Do you think maybe... before you take me home that we could finish what we started back there?"

My heartbeat accelerated as I choked out a reply, "If you want to."

"I do..."

Carefully, I moved in closer. He placed his hands on my pecs and stood on his tiptoes. I licked my dry lips as his eyes tried to anticipate my next move. "Is something wrong?" He offered.

"No... I've just never kissed anyone before."

"Neither have I," he whispered.

We moved a little closer, "We honestly don't have to if you're not ready?"

He rolled his eyes and placed his hands on my cheeks, "Oh for God's sakes."

Then before I could reply, I felt his lips pressed against mine. We held them together for what seemed like forever when he finally released me and started toward the four-wheeler. I just stood there in a goofy daze before flashing a cheesy smile and playfully running to catch up with him. On the way home, we didn't say a word. He just held on and rested against my back until we pulled up in front of his trailer.

As he got off, he stood by me for a moment before speaking. "I had a really nice time."

"So did I."

"Same time tomorrow?"

"Definitely."

He started to back away when I shouted, Wait!"

Without a word, I dismounted and walked right up to him. He was staring up at me with his big brown eyes when I positioned my hand behind his neck and slowly leaned in. He rose on his tiptoes to meet me, and our lips met in a long, sensual kiss before I pulled away. "See you tomorrow," I whispered.

He just nodded and started to walk away... almost like he was drunk. I hit the gas and rushed to make it back to Grandpa's before the sun was gone. On the way, I couldn't help but feel like I was on top of the world. I could feel the cool, late-summer wind, rushing through my hair. I could feel it caressing my face. My heart and soul were howling in celebration of the moments we just shared. I'd just kissed my first boy and nothing or no one had ever felt better than I did right now.

PART TWO

WAYLON

Over the next few days, we'd fallen into a routine. During the day, we'd do our chores and whatever was required from our folks, then in the evenings we'd meet for some quality time. Some nights by the creek at my place, others in the junkyard at his Papaw's. Come Friday night, mom had picked up a double shift and given Scooter and I permission to stay out a little later than usual.

She said we didn't have to be home until 9, which was about an hour before she got home. I'd spent a good portion of the afternoon obsessing about what to wear and wondering what he had planned. The night before, he'd told me to leave it to him. Now, all I have to do is wait, but sometimes waiting is the hardest part.

SCOOTER

Grandpa still hadn't caught on that Waylon and I were more than just friends. I'm honestly not sure how he would react. In some ways, he can be very open-minded, but he's still from a far different generation than Waylon and me. I think, for now, the best option is to keep things on the down-low and take a, don't ask don't tell, approach. If we're careful, then he won't feel the need to ask any questions. Like tonight, I'd thought about it long and hard and decided it was high time I take Waylon on a proper date. We'd get some cheeseburgers and fries from the country store and find a quiet place to enjoy them.

Even with all the good things going on, I have been worried about him and his mom. He told me that his dad came into the diner the other day looking for her, asking about him, and trying to get Loretta to let him come by. I told him that I thought it would be a really bad idea but his mom seems convinced that he's straightened himself out. Little does he know, I'm quite familiar with having an addict in the family. You see, I had an older brother named Bubba Ray who overdosed a few years back.

It tore my family apart. To be honest, I've known my parents have been on the verge of divorce for a while now. Dad blames himself for Bubba's death. I think that's why he's been so hard on me... he's just afraid of losing me too. What he doesn't know is if I learned anything from Bubba's death, it was life is short and the checks we write today will eventually have to be paid one way or another tomorrow.

He had it all, friends, girlfriends, popularity, a football scholarship to the University of Kentucky. However, he threw it all away at a party where his friends thought it would be fun to try some new stuff. They shot up, snorted, and drank anything they could get their hands on. In the morning, they couldn't wake him up.

The thing I remember most about him was his loyalty. I think he knew I was gay. He used to catch me checking out his friends and never said a word. A few times when I was out with him around town, he even asked if I had anything I wanted to talk to him about. At the time, I declined, but now I wish I would have told him everything. He always used to say, "Bro's are bro's forever and nothing would ever change that."

Tonight, I'm wearing his blue jean jacket because I'm a little afraid. I'm afraid of what might happen after our date. I'm afraid things might be moving too fast with Waylon and me. It's nights like this that I wish he was here to talk to. In my heart, I know he wouldn't have cared either way if I was straight or gay. He'd just want me to be happy. He'd probably have made some joke about not stealing or flirting with his friends. Then, he'd have tousled my hair and wrestled me to the ground. He was such a douche. Yet, as I stand here in the mirror looking at my misty eyes, wearing my best jeans and button-up shirt, I miss him… I love him. Sometimes when the moment's just right, I can still smell his BOD body spray.

There's no more time to waste, I have a date… my first official date with a boy. I only hope I say and do the right things to let him know that I really care a lot about him. In fact, I think he's the one. I just hope I have the balls to tell him.

WAYLON

I'd just set my empty glass in the sink when I heard a car out front. I rushed to the door in hopes that it was Scooter coming to pick me up. Unfortunately, what I found was my dad in a beat-up duster. He was wearing his old leather jacket, ripped-up jeans, and looked like he hadn't showered in a few days. "Dad, what are you doing here?"

He paused and looked a little shocked that someone was here, "Your mama said you were out with a friend?"

"He's not here yet but does she know you're here?"

"We're still married," he snapped, "I can come by here anytime I want."

"Not after the last time," I fired back.

He stormed up the steps, "You watch your mouth, boy. I can do anything I damn well please."

I backed away, "But, she's got a restraining order! Dad, please just go." I held up my hands, "I don't want any trouble."

He spread his arms, "What the hell are you gonna do about it?"

The sudden realization that I was backed into the corner of the porch and it was too far to jump to escape dawned on me. I knew he could see I was afraid. He softened his stance, then ran his fingers through his hair. His hands were trembling as he continued, "Look, I just need a little money to get what I need and I'll go. You got any money or anything I can sell?"

"No dad, honestly I don't..."

"You're lying," he growled.

Then, before I could say anything else he lunged for me. I shouted, "Please daddy... please don't hit me."

He managed to wrestle the wallet from my back pocket and checked the inside to find it empty "This is bullshit," he roared.

He threw it down then snatched me up by the collar of my shirt, "I know you've got some money somewhere. I've seen you rolling around the hollow with that Creech boy from down the road."

I was in tears as I cried out, "I promise I ain't got no money, daddy. I swear to God."

During the commotion, I hadn't even noticed that Scooter had pulled up in his Grandad's pickup. He rushed onto the porch and shouted, "Let him go!"

Dad released me and I collapsed in a ball to the ground. When he turned around, Scooter was standing with his fists balled, "Why don't you pick on somebody your own size?"

Dad laughed, "Who do you think you are, little boy."

"I ain't your boy and I ain't little."

He danced around, "Alright, big boy. Let's see what you're made of. I'll even let you have the first shot."

As always, dad wasn't true to his word. He took a swing at Scooter and missed. While he was trying to regain his composure, Scooter took a swing and caught dad right across the jaw. Dad stumbled and fell while Scooter rushed to me and took my hand, "Come on! Let's get the hell out of here!"

As we rushed to get away, I felt a hand grip my ankle and a voice growl from the floor of the deck, "Get back here you little punk, and fight like a man!"

I screamed and shouted, "Help Scooter help!" I struggled to get free for a moment before Scooter stomped dad's wrist with his foot and shouted in reply, "Let him go! Let him fucking go!"

Hand in hand we rushed to his grandad's truck and piled in before Scooter hit the gas. We did a donut through the yard and sped up the driveway. At the end, he paused for a minute and met my gaze, "Are you alright?"

I nodded silently, still a little shaken from the whole encounter and he took my hand. Then, Scooter hit the gas again and we disappeared around the bend headed toward his place. When we got there, we both ran inside and he called the police. I told him the address and when he got off the phone, he rushed to me and wrapped his arms around my neck. I started to cry as he kissed my head and whispered "You ain't got to be scared anymore. I've got you now and I'm never gonna let anyone hurt you again."

There in his grandpa's living room, we held for what seemed like an eternity before separating. When we did, he placed his hands on the sides of my face and examined me, "Did he hit you?"

I shook my head no, as he threw his arms around me again. There, in his arms, for the first time in my life, I felt safe. I could feel the coarse denim of his jacket on my fingertips. I could feel the muscles in his biceps bulge. I could feel his heart pounding. I lifted slightly to meet his gaze. His expression was hard and pensive, "I swear to God if I ever see him again I'll kill him."

I shook my head, "It's not worth it... he's not worth it. This is how he's always been. Besides, I'm safe now thanks to you."

He forced a smile, "I'm just sorry I didn't get there sooner."

"You came... that's all that matters. You came and you rescued me!" Silence lingered for a moment before I lowered my gaze, "Thank you... no one's ever done anything like that for me."

I lifted my eyes to find his but found them lowered and closed. "Listen, Waylon. There's something important I need to say. I just couldn't find the words. I've been thinking about it all day and after what just happened, I need you to know that I... I... love you."

My lips curved to a shy smile as he continued, "I've never met anyone like you... so sweet and kind. How someone as precious as you could come from a brut like that is beyond me... but I love you Waylon Evarts and I would die for you."

"Oh, Scooter," I exhaled.

Then without another word, I met his lips in a kiss. It started out slow and sweet, then I opened mine to invite him in. He took the hint and gently pushed his tongue inside. A battle ensued. We shuffled to unbutton shirts and discard clothes. He'd taken a momentary detour from my lips to nibble my neck. I was panting and moaning in his ear as our bodies gently lapped at one another's like ripples in a pond. "When does your grandpa get back?"

"Not until after last call," he exhaled.

We tumbled onto a dated plaid sofa, stole a few kisses, then separated long enough to undo our pants. He stood to let his fall to the floor, then yanked mine from the bottom. Once they were off, I tugged down my underwear and watched as he did the same. His wanton cock was fully alert and waving around like a flag when he melted onto my body and began ravishing my lips and neck again. I was hard as a rock too, and gently leaking precum the further down this road we went.

SCOOTER

I couldn't get enough. Seeing him so vulnerable and clinging to me set my heart and soul on fire. I needed to show him how much I loved him. I needed to show him how far I would go. I needed to feel his naked skin pressed against mine. I needed to taste his lips and know they were mine. This thirst I had for a guy could only be quenched by this hillbilly angel. Aw shit, we'd gone buck wild and there was no turning back now.

You'd think with me being this hard wall of country muscle, that I'd be a top. To his surprise and yours maybe, I had decided, I think, I would like to be the bottom. I took his cock in my mouth and started suckin' for all I was worth. I'd never done it before but the concept was pretty simple. He was whimpering and moaning in ecstasy the faster and deeper I went. Then, after a while of that, I rose up and whispered, "Take me!"

"Take you where?" He said playfully.

I jerked my head, "You know, back there, inside of me."

His eyes widened, "Are you sure?"

"Mm-hmm, it's all I can think about at night."

"But wouldn't you rather...?"

I shook my head, "Maybe someday, but I want you to be my first."

"Alright," he grinned.

I took my position, legs spread and hands on the back of the sofa as he jerked himself harder. I closed my eyes and grinned. I couldn't wait to know what it felt like to have him inside of me. Just before he went in, I moaned, "Wait," then spit in my hand and massaged it into my hole. "Now... easy."

He poised himself outside. I could feel myself pulsing to welcome him. Just as I said, he started slow and let out little breaths as he went deeper and deeper. "Oh...God... yes..." I groaned.

Once he was fully inserted, he lay on my back and gripped my abs. His little ginger thrusts were causing my cock to bounce with the rhythm of his fuck. God, it felt so good. I'd dreamed of this moment since we met and couldn't stand it anymore. I took my cock into hand and began stroking away as his pace accelerated. There wasn't a lot of exchange of words, just pleasure-laden breaths and sighs as we approached our destination.

We'd been going at it good for about ten minutes when he shouted, "Scooter... Scooter, I'm gonna shoot."

"Shoot it, baby, give me all of your sweet cum."

With a shout and a few grunts from him, I started to fill up. The way he kept going even after he'd come sent me over the edge. I let out an animalistic growl and watched as stream after stream of love blasted out of my penis and onto the couch below us. "Damn," I chuckled. "Shit, it's everywhere!"

He laughed too and we rushed to separate and get ourselves and things cleaned up before someone caught us. Afterward, we took a seat on the towel-covered sofa and lazily held hands as we talked about how incredible it was.

WAYLON

How this suddenly changed from one of the worst nights of my life to one of the best is beyond me. Scooter had turned on the TV and we'd gotten distracted by some western that was on when both of our stomachs growled simultaneously. We turned and glanced at one another before smiling, "Sounds like dinnertime," he crooned.

"What do you have in mind," I replied.

He thought for a minute, "Well, I was gonna take you to the country store but they're closed now. We could just have some chips and sandwiches. Grandpa always has stuff like that around here."

"I'm game," I grinned.

He stood and led the way to the kitchen. I followed and got lost watching his butt shift in his jeans. It was difficult not to get turned on again knowing what it looks and feels like. It was hard as stone and while we were engaged in our act of passion, it felt like I had one of those Chinese finger traps latched on my cock.

In the kitchen, Scooter starter pulling packages of lunch meat from his Grandpa's old Almond Gold fridge. He sat them on the counter and grabbed a loaf of bread with the top folded over nearby. He was smiling as we took some paper plates and began making our humble meal in silence. "Mayonnaise?"

"Bleh, never cared for it!"

"Neither have I."

I grinned at his response and our shared dislike. "I will take some mustard if you have it?"

He went to the fridge and pulled some out, "It ain't Grey Poupon but it's alright."

I held up my pinky in mockery and he chuckled. Once we were done, we made our way back to the living room and started watching the western that was on earlier; Two Mules for Sister Sara. Every once in a while, we would glance at one another and look kind of shy. In my mind, I couldn't help but think of how nice this was. An odd flash to the future told me that this was how life with him was gonna be, and I couldn't ask for more.

Unfortunately, as happy as I was now, being poor has taught me one thing. If something can go wrong, it will. My mind couldn't help but wonder if we were just living a heartbreak dream that we were destined to wake up from. It's hard for straight couples to make it in today's world. What made us so special that life might take it easier on us? Still, I couldn't worry about that right now. Right now, I just wanted to enjoy this time with him.

At some point, after we'd eaten, we succumbed to sleep... right there in his Grandpa's living room. The sound of the front door closing woke us up. We'd been snuggled up on the couch... my head on his chest when a tall, graying, man entered. "It's past midnight, Scooter, you best get that boy home."

We were still trying to rub the sleep from our eyes and make like nothing was going on when he responded with a nervous, "Yes sir!"

In the truck, I couldn't help but ask, "Do you think he thought anything about us on the couch like that?"

"Don't know," he replied dryly.

"He must have," I mumbled, "I didn't even hear him come in."

"Well, whether he did or didn't, we can't erase it now. He's pretty cool for an old man but I hope he's too drunk to remember in the morning. Either way, don't worry about it. I'll deal with him. Now, what do we tell your mom?"

"That we fell asleep," I shrugged, "She'll still be freaked out as hell but at least she knows I'm with you."

"I'm not sure if that's a good thing or not," he smirked.

I shook my head and we continued in silence until he turned down the road to my house. I knew he was just as nervous as I was, especially after what happened earlier.

Mom was sitting on the porch in a rocking chair but got up when we pulled in. She rushed to the truck and her voice was tinged with panic. "I was worried sick."

Scooter apologized as she continued, "What's Waylon's dad's car doing here?"

I swallowed hard but couldn't find my words. In between us, Scooter took my hand and spoke valiantly, "He was here when I came to pick up Waylon. He had him by the collar and I punched him!"

"Oh, God," mom rubbed her face. Turning to me she said, "Did he hurt you?"

"No ma'am... Scooter got here just in time."

Her tone softened a little as she turned her gaze to Scooter. "Thank you, thank you for protecting him."

Scooter replied, "It was nothin'... nothin' at all, ma'am."

Mom asked, "Where is he now?"

"We called the cops once I got him back to my Grandpa's", Scooter said

Mom replied, "Well, at least he didn't hurt

anyone or take anything this time."

She stretched out her hand to take Scooters. "I can't thank you enough for watching out for my baby."

"Well... I am rather fond of him," Scooter grinned.

"Now," mom's tone hardened again, "What happened that you boys couldn't get here when I asked?"

I swallowed hard as Scooter took charge again, "Oh, we got caught up watching a western after dinner and fell asleep. I'm real sorry."

Mom was silent for a minute, holding firm to her hard expression before she smiled, "Considering what happened, I can look past it tonight. Waylon, tell him goodnight and get inside."

"Yes ma'am."

She disappeared inside the trailer as Scooter turned to me and smiled, "That went better than I thought."

"Right... she must really like you to not go wildcat crazy."

"That's a good thing, right?"

I nodded silently as I squeezed his hand then leaned in for a kiss. It was long, slow, and sensual. I never wanted it to end. As we slowly pulled away, he rested his forehead against mine and sighed, "It gets harder every time to say goodbye."

"Hopefully," I mumbled, "There'll come a day where we never have to say goodbye."

"From your mouth to God's ears," he

chuckled.

As I got out of the truck and headed to the porch, I glanced back to see him watching me. Once I was safely behind the screen door, he started up the truck and turned around in the yard. I was standing there like a little kid with my hand pressed against the window glass. As he passed, he tooted the horn, then sped off into the night,

I turned around, to find mom sitting on the sofa with a cup of coffee. "You really like him don't you?"

"Yes, very much."

"And he appears to like you too."

"I think so."

"That's why it makes what I have to tell you so much harder."

"What is it?"

She took a deep breath, "I've got some good news... depending on your perspective."

"What? What is it?"

"Well, you remember Jodie Holloway. She used to work with me a while ago at the diner."

"Vaguely."

"Anyways, she came in tonight to ask if I'd be interested in being the manager of a little Huddle House franchise she's opening up down in Pennington Gap. Apparently, her husband passed and left her a lot of money."

"Virginia?"

"Yes, it's about forty minutes or so south of here."

"But... what about the trailer and land? Gramp and Nan wouldn't want us to sell it!"

Mom shook her head, "I know. However, I can't take care of it myself and you know this old trailer is fallin' down around us."

I stood, "But you always said we would fix it up. You said it would always be in the family!"

"I know," mama added sadly before lifting her eyes to meet mine. "Baby, this is our chance to get out of here... to make something of ourselves... to have a good life. I thought you'd be happy!"

"What about Scooter?"

"You boys can still see each other. It's not all that far over the mountain."

I started to back away as panic invaded my expression, "No, no we can't and you know it!"

Mama finally stood, "Calm down, baby, we'll figure something out, I promise!"

Tears were rolling down my cheeks as I shouted, "You can't make me give him up. I love him, mama! Do you hear me? I love him I said!"

She stretched out her arms with tear-filled eyes to offer me a hug. "Waylon, trust me I understand, I honestly do."

"You'll never understand," I jerked away, "we're gonna get married... we're gonna have a good life." My voice fell to a whimper, "He's my everything."

She met my gaze again before I ran out the screen door. She ran after me shouting, "Waylon, wait! Wait!"

I was already down the stairs and on my four-wheeler when she reached the bottom. "Waylon!"

The last thing I saw when I turned around was her crying and shouting, "Baby, please come back… you're all I got left."

Through the sea of tears flooding my eyes, I was only able to make out the road enough to see the edges. However, my heart knew which direction I was going. I needed to get to Scooter. My heart needed to get to Scooter. I needed to get to him fast so we could make a plan. There was one sure-fire way to make sure we never had to say goodbye… runaway. Far away from this wicked little town where nothing or no one could ever hurt us again.

SCOOTER

Grandpa had fallen asleep in his lazy boy recliner by the time I got back. I grabbed a throw from the back of the couch and tossed it over him before going back outside. I was feeling some kind of way after what Waylon said back at his place. *"Hopefully, there would come a day where we never had to say goodbye."*

There was a star shining in the clear early autumn sky as I turned my gaze upward and sighed. My mind temporarily drifted to mom and dad and what they'd think of Waylon. If he were a girl, they would love him. He's so warm, and sweet, and kind. Unfortunately, because he was a boy, they'd never accept it. In their efforts to keep me alive, they'd held on too tightly and I'd slipped away.

I knew when they sent me to Grandpa's they were done. They hadn't spoken to me all summer except on my birthday when they stopped by to give me a pair of jeans and a Realtree shirt from the Dollar General store. In my heart, I wished and prayed they'd accept me for who I am but I know that'll never happen. Besides, when that counselor suggested I go to conversion therapy, they wanted me to. I don't think I'll ever get over that. Instead of loving me for who I am, they would rather me change everything I am to be the person they want me to be.

I sighed as I sat down in an old rocking chair and got lost deeper in my thoughts. The sound of an engine approaching snapped me out of the spell. I stood and squinted as the headlights changed directions and came right at me. My heart danced when I realized it was Waylon. However, I was baffled as to why he was back so late. When he turned the motor off and dimmed the light, I noticed he'd been crying. I immediately rushed to him and wrapped my arms around his neck. "What happened? What's wrong?"

He sniffled in my chest and whined, "Oh, Scooter. I don't know what to do."

I lifted him so I could look into his eyes. "Tell me what happened."

He wiped his nose on his sleeve as he continued. "Mama got offered a job."

"Hey, that's great!"

"No..." he replied solemnly. "It's forty minutes south of here in Pennington Gap."

"Oh."

I looked away and attempted to regain my composure. "So… what does that mean for us?"

"That's the thing… I've decided I'm not going. You see, I'm no better than my daddy."

"Don't say things like that!"

"No, honestly. You're my drug Scooter. From the first time you kissed me I got high, and I don't ever wanna come down. I'm addicted to you, Scooter. Do you hear me? I'm addicted to you and I'd rather die than have to say goodbye to you."

"Oh, Waylon," I whimpered.

We embraced again. This time harder than ever before. We were literally holding on for our lives and crying our eyes out as he wailed. "If I can't be with you, then I don't want to be alive. I need you!"

"Oh, Waylon, I need you too and I don't know what to say."

He pulled away, "Say you'll run away. We can pack a bag and be in Kingsport in an hour or two."

"I… I… I'm not sure that's a good idea. Grandpa is old and I can't just up and leave him."

"Oh, Scooter, please? We can make it. I know we can. I've got a couple of dollars in my piggy bank for gas. All we got to do is make it over the state line and they'll never find us. We could camp out in the truck, get jobs, then eventually we can find a room at a weekly hotel where we can live. It won't be easy but at least we'll be together."

"Can I think about it?"

"There's no time," he cried. "If we're gonna

do this, we have to leave tonight while everyone's asleep."

"Okay," I nodded. "You go back home and make like everything's alright. I'll pack and come to get you in an hour."

In a passionate rush, he met my lips in a kiss. I released him and exhaled, "Go, go pack and I'll be there before long."

He rushed back to his four-wheeler and hopped on. Once he was gone, I rushed inside and to my room. As I was throwing clothes and stuff into a bag, I couldn't help but wonder if this was the best idea. All I know is I love him and can't bear to think we couldn't see each other every day. Also, we'd had sex. I was a virgin no more and that sacred part of my boyhood now belonged to him. For as long as I live, I'd never be able to erase the fact that we became one.

My heart was pounding as I tip-toed up the hall and past Grandpa. For a moment, he stirred, then let out a snore before I continued toward the front door. With a ragged breath and a glance around the room, I whispered, "Goodbye," then carefully shut the door behind me.

Outside, I opened the door to the truck and threw my backpack behind the seat. Just as I was about to get in, a flicker of light on the front porch caught my attention. "Where you going?"

"To pick up Waylon."

"And from there?"

"Well, his mama's gettin' a new job down in

Pennington. That means he'll have to move and we won't be able to see each other anymore."

Grandpa shifted his weight, "I take it you boys are involved?"

"Yes, yes sir we are."

"Well, there ain't nothin' wrong with that. It's your life and you're a grown boy."

I was amazed at how well he was taking this when he lowered his tone, "However, I wish you'd reconsider. I've found in my years that making a permanent decision based on temporary circumstances is never a good idea."

"Well..."

"Why don't you give it until the morning? You know how hard it is to drive through these mountains at night."

He stepped closer and placed his hand on my shoulder. "I know we haven't really seen eye to eye on things, but the truth is I love ya, son. I don't want to see you struggling to make it... wherever the hell it is you boys are thinkin' about runnin' off to."

"Kingsport."

"Kingsport," he nodded. "Fancy."

I started to cry as he tightened his grip on my shoulder and pulled me in. "Shh."

"But I love him, Papa. I don't want him to think I abandoned him."

"You're not, you're just giving him time to reconsider. That's all."

I pulled away and sniffled as he continued, "Now, let's stop all this blubberin' and go inside.

Things will look clearer in the light of day."

I nodded silently before reaching into the truck to get my backpack. Then, with Grandpa's arm around my neck, we went back inside.

WAYLON

I waited for him. I waited all night, but he never came. I was devasted to say the least. I could hear mom making coffee just down the hall and rose up in bed. After checking the alarm clock, I realized it was nearly noon. What was she doing home? She normally leaves for work about fifteen minutes until nine, so she can be to work on time. I scurried to get dressed and stepped out to hear her talking to someone just outside the front door.

I was still groggy and rubbing my eyes when I stepped onto the porch to find Scooter and his Grandpa sitting there. I immediately frowned as Scooter rose, "Waylon!"

I turned and went back inside but he followed. "Waylon, wait! I can explain!"

"I think you not showing up said everything."

I was headed back to my room when I felt his hand grip my shoulder. I spun around and tried to shake him off but he just placed his other hand on the opposite side and growled, "Listen to me... I can explain."

I diverted my gaze as he continued, "The reason I didn't show up, is because my Papa caught me and convinced me it wasn't a good idea."

"Shouldn't that have been for us to decide?"

"You don't understand. He wanted me to wait until the morning so we'd have time to make sure we were doing the right thing. He even offered to take us if I waited."

"So, is that why he's here?"

"Not exactly. You see, when we got here and Grandpa told your mom what we were planning, she had another idea."

LORETTA

"Do you think he's told Waylon yet?"

"Hard to tell, your boy seemed pretty upset to see Scooter after not showing up last night."

"I'm just so thankful you managed to talk him out of it. I would have been worried sick to have woken up and found him gone."

"I know. I'm just thankful nature called or else I'd have never heard him sneaking out."

"Well, I hope this doesn't get him into any trouble but I think it's the best idea for everyone."

"Oh, his folks won't mind. They barely pay that boy any attention now that he's older. They didn't when he was younger. Ray was their pride and joy."

"Poor, Ray. I remember seeing his picture in the paper after the games."

"He was a good boy… just got roped into that party scene and couldn't dig his way out."

"I'm so glad Waylon dropped out when he did. These schools around here are just as bad as the streets."

"You're right, there."

"Well, I can't lie, the anticipation is killing me. I just wished he'd come on out here and be his normal, happy, self again."

WAYLON

"What do you mean mom didn't go to work yesterday?"

"Waylon, she didn't want to tell you that she got a sign-on bonus and money to move, from Ms. Jodie. She went down there yesterday to rent a new house!"

"Rent?"

"It's only temporary, but it has three bedrooms."

"What do we need three bedrooms for? Dad's not coming back to live with us, is he?"

Scooter rolled his eyes and exhaled, "No... try again."

"But I don't understand."

He took my hand and lead me to the front porch, where his Grandpa and my mom were anxiously waiting. "Well," mom said to Scooter, "Did you tell him?"

"He's having some trouble wrapping his head around it."

Mom stood and took my hands, "Honey, you don't have to say goodbye to Scooter. Y'all don't even have to be apart. I rented a three-bedroom house so Scooter could come live with us. It'll be easier for him to get a job down there, plus he can help us keep things up until we can all buy something."

"What?"

Scooter placed his hands on the sides of my face, "We're gonna be livin' together, stupid!"

A feeling of warmth and happiness washed over me as I threw my arms around his neck. "Do you really mean it?"

"Of course, I do."

After a moment, I pulled away from Scooter and threw my arms around mom. She stroked my hair and whispered. "See, it's like I always said, we're gonna make it someday... and today is that day."

I started to cry as she whispered again, "No one will ever have to say goodbye... not now... not ever. Except for the reader.

"But what will they do?"

"They'll go on living their life with the hope that someday things will turn out alright for themselves. Even when it seems like everything's going wrong, somehow, someway, everything will be okay."

A few months after mom started at the Huddle House, she got me a job as a cook. Now, we work together and are closer than ever. Scooter even got on at an oil change place and is doing really well. Since his birthday is so close to Christmas, his grandpa gave him his gift birthday gift early.

While all of us were getting settled in and working, he had Scooter's favorite truck from the junkyard towed and restored. One day Scooter got home from work to find the truck parked in the driveway with a big bow on top. He cried and immediately hugged his Grandpa. After all kinds of thanks and more tears of happiness, he offered to take me for a ride.

We took it up to the old homeplace and sat by the creek for the longest time before he rose to one knee and asked if I would marry him. Now, we've come full circle and hope to save up some money to rent our own place very soon. No matter how hard we try it's kind of hard to make love when she's just down the hall from us.

It seemed kind of crazy but at first, when we all moved into the new house, she wouldn't let him stay in the same room as me. Eventually, mom did some soul-searching and decided it was alright for us to be in the same room. She could see just how much we loved each other. Mom has decided that as soon as she sells the old homeplace, she would help us out to build up our savings. Until then, we're just living the good life and working.

Shortly after Christmas, we received a call from an investigator stating that daddy had died from an overdose at the shop he was working at. Everyone we talked to told us he'd been off the stuff for a while but unfortunately, however long he is off, he just keeps going back when he has the opportunity and gets high again. The police in Harlan are currently investigating the guy who sold the stuff to him. They think it might have been laced with fentanyl because it was listed as the cause of death.

My grandparents from dad's side had disowned him a long time ago and didn't speak to us too often. Thankfully, they did offer to pay half the funeral costs. He had been such a distant part of our family we just had him cremated and then had his ashes sprinkled around the old shop at the home-place he used to love when he was right. Life is no joke, it's a roller coaster ride of emotions and heart-break. Unfortunately, some never get off the roller coaster. They just keep going round and round, up and down, until they die.

I was on that same ride. That is, until the day a roughneck boy named, Scooter Creech rode up on his four-wheeler and swept me off my feet. It's nice to know, that despite all the bad things in life, I never have to wake up from that heartbreak dream I was living in right after we met. So, with all of my heart and all of the love a boy can give, I hope you find your heartbreak dream and you never have to wake up from it.

THE END

FOR MORE BOOKS BY DANIEL ELIJAH SANDERFER, FOLLOW HIM ON AMAZON. ALSO, PLEASE FEEL FREE TO JOIN HIS FACEBOOK GROUP SANDERFER'S SOCIALITES.

Printed in Great Britain
by Amazon

83030141R00037